For all my South African friends, especially Sam,
who introduced me to the story—A. D.

For my wonderful wife, Keegan Blankenaar, and
Piet Grobler—this book would be impossible
without you—D. B.

Published by Charlesbridge
9 Galen Street, Watertown, MA 02472
(617) 926-0329 • www.charlesbridge.com

First published in the UK © Tiny Owl Publishing Ltd 2019
Text © Alan Durant 2019
Illustrations © Dale Blankenaar 2019

Library of Congress Cataloging-in-Publication Data
Names: Durant, Alan, 1958– author. | Blankenaar, Dale, illustrator.
Title: Quill soup / Alan Durant ; illustrated by Dale Blankenaar.
Other titles: Stone soup. English.
Description: First US edition. | Watertown, MA : Charlesbridge, 2020. |
  "First published in the UK Tiny Owl Publishing Ltd 2019"—Copyright
  page. | Summary: In this African version of the traditional folktale Stone
  Soup, Noko the porcupine tricks the other well-fed but selfish animals
  into sharing their food with him and the whole village.
Identifiers: LCCN 2019014848 (print) | LCCN 2019019422 (ebook) |
  ISBN 9781632899231 (ebook) | ISBN 9781623541477 (hardcover)
Subjects: LCSH: Porcupines—Folklore—Juvenile fiction. |
  Animals—Folklore—Juvenile fiction. | Soups—Folklore—Juvenile fiction. |
  Sharing—Folklore—Juvenile fiction. | Folklore—Africa. | CYAC: Folklore. |
  LCGFT: Folk tales.
Classification: LCC PZ8.1.D927 (ebook) | LCC PZ8.1.D927 Qu 2020 (print) |
  DDC 398.2 [E] —dc23
LC record available at https://lccn.loc.gov/2019014848

Printed in China
(hc) 10 9 8 7 6 5 4 3 2 1

Text type set in Museo Sans 500 by Jos Buivenga
Printed by 1010 Printing International Limited in Huizhou,
  Guangdong, China
Production supervision by Brian G. Walker
Designed by Jacqueline Noelle Cote

QUILL SOUP

SOUP

A STONE SOUP STORY

Alan Durant

Illustrated by
Dale Blankenaar

ini **Charlesbridge**

Noko the porcupine was hungry
and tired. He'd been traveling through
the Valley of a Thousand Hills and
hadn't eaten for days.

He saw a small village ahead,
and his spirits lifted.
"Food and shelter at last,"
he thought.

Meanwhile in the village, the animals caught sight of Noko.

"There's a stranger coming!" squeaked Monkey.
"Quick, run to your homes!" shouted Meerkat.

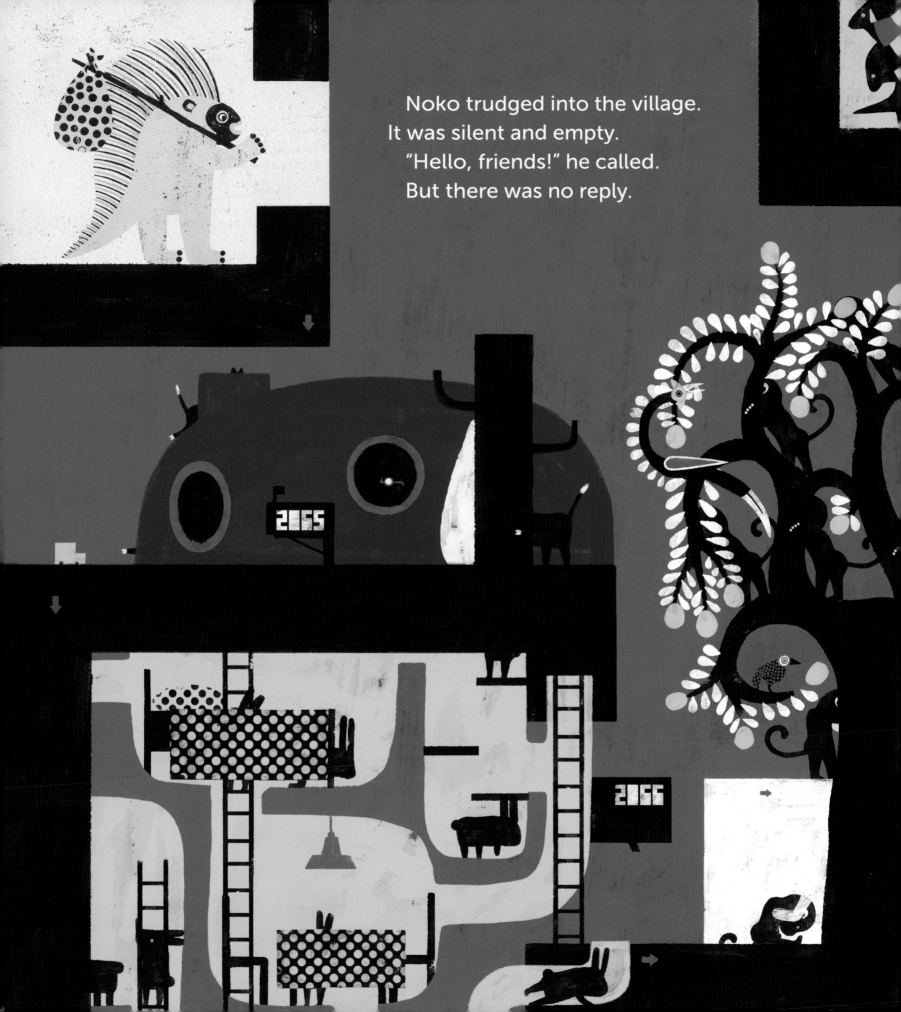

Noko trudged into the village.
It was silent and empty.
"Hello, friends!" he called.
But there was no reply.

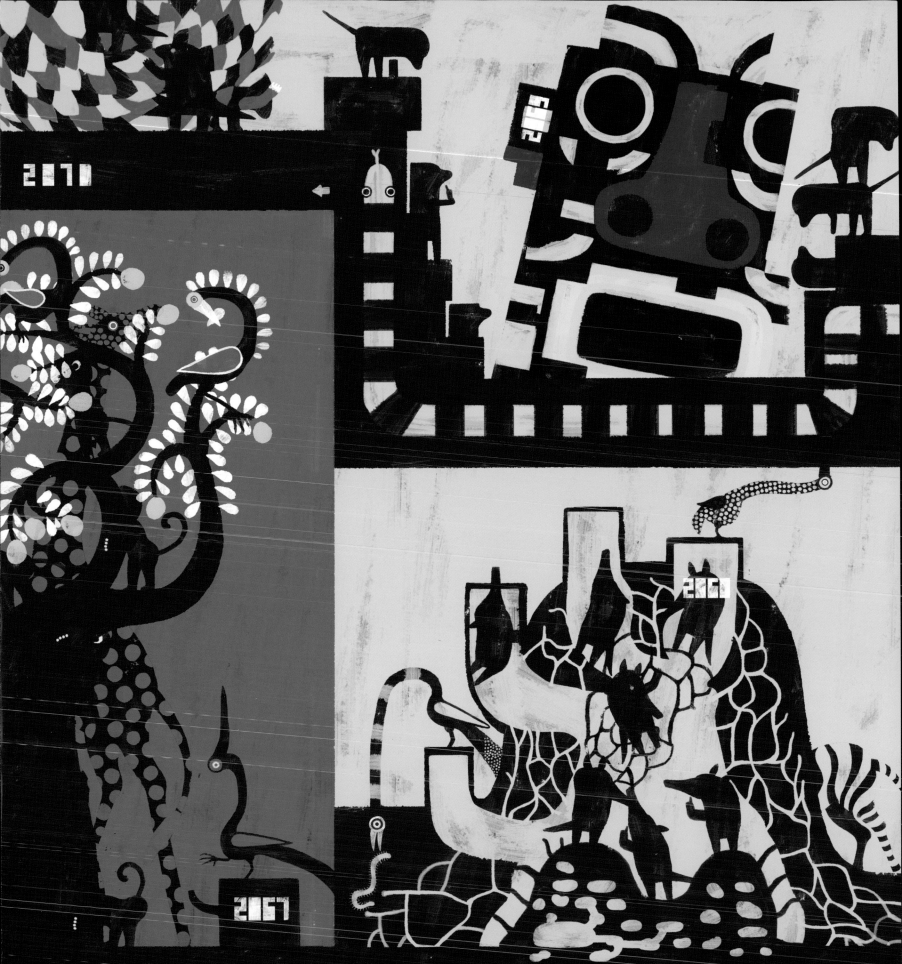

Noko went to the first house and tapped on the door.

"Yes?" asked Warthog.

"I've traveled a long way, and I'm very hungry," said Noko. "Do you have anything I can eat?"

Warthog shook her big head. "I'm sorry," she replied. "I ate a big lunch, and all my food is gone."

Noko knocked at the next house.
"How can I help?" asked Rabbit.
"Please, I need some food,"
said Noko.

"So do I!" Rabbit exclaimed.
"My greedy brother came to
visit and ate all my food. I have
nothing left."

Noko knocked at Monkey's door.
"Yes, what is it?" Monkey asked.
"I wonder if you have any food to spare for a poor traveler?" Noko inquired.

"We are *poor* villagers," Monkey grumbled. "We don't have any spare food."

So Noko went to Aardvark's house . . .

. . . and Meerkat's house,

and Pangolin's house.

But he came away hungry. All of them said they didn't have any food.

By this time Noko was very tired and very hungry indeed. But his brain was as sharp as the quills on his back. He could see from the villagers' sleek coats and rounded bellies that they were lying.

He knew they had food. How was he going to get some?

He sat and thought, and after a while he came up with a plan.

"I wonder if I might have a little fire and a large pot of water," he asked the villagers.

"Of course," they replied.
They couldn't refuse him that.

Noko put the pot on the fire so the water could boil.

"It seems I shall have to make my own food." He sighed. "I will make quill soup."

He plucked three quills from his back and dropped them into the big pot.

"But surely the quills are too hard and sharp to eat," Warthog said.

"Wait and see! Soon they will soften and release flavor to make a delicious soup," Noko explained.

He bent over the pot and dipped in a paw. He licked his paw and nodded. "*Mmmm*, tasty," he said. "Just how His Majesty likes it."

"You've met the king?" squeaked Meerkat.

2067

"Many times," Noko said casually. "I always make him quill soup. He loves it."

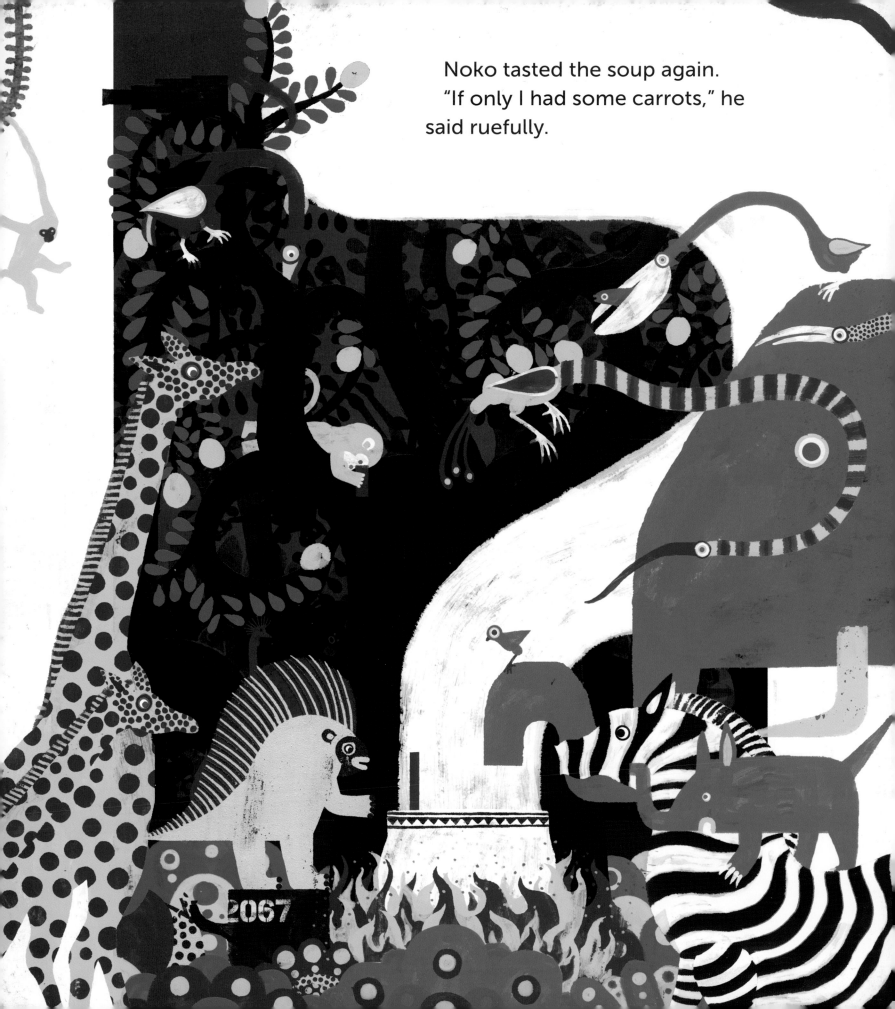

Noko tasted the soup again.
"If only I had some carrots," he
said ruefully.

Rabbit's ears shot up. He wanted to taste this quill soup that was fit for a king.

"I think my greedy brother may have left a carrot or two," he blurted out.

He hopped away to fetch them.

Noko added the carrots to the water and tasted the soup again.

"Lovely," he announced. "Of course, the king likes mealies in his quill soup."

"I've got mealies!" squealed Meerkat. She ran away to find them.

Each time Noko tasted the soup, there
was something that needed to be added:
beans, peas, potatoes, spinach . . .
And then the things appeared within
moments, as if by magic.

Now Noko's soup was thick and rich.
Once again he tasted it.
"Perfect," he declared. "Unless . . . I don't
suppose anyone has a few worms?"
Pangolin did!

NOKO told the villagers to fetch their bowls.
"There's plenty of soup to share," he said.
And share they did! They drank bowl after
bowl of the delicious soup in the firelight
until the big pot was empty.

Noko sat back, looked up at the stars, and yawned.
"I wonder if you might have a hole where I could sleep?" he asked.

"A hole!" cried Monkey. "For someone who has cooked delicious quill soup for the king?"

"And who has the generosity to share the soup with strangers?" piped in Aardvark.

"No, my friend," said Monkey. "You, Noko, shall have the very best bed in my house."

"You're too kind." Noko smiled.

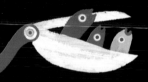

Before they went to their beds, Noko and the villagers sang together, shared stories, and danced in the moonlight.

Later on, with a full tummy and
a happy heart, Noko the traveler
went to sleep at last.

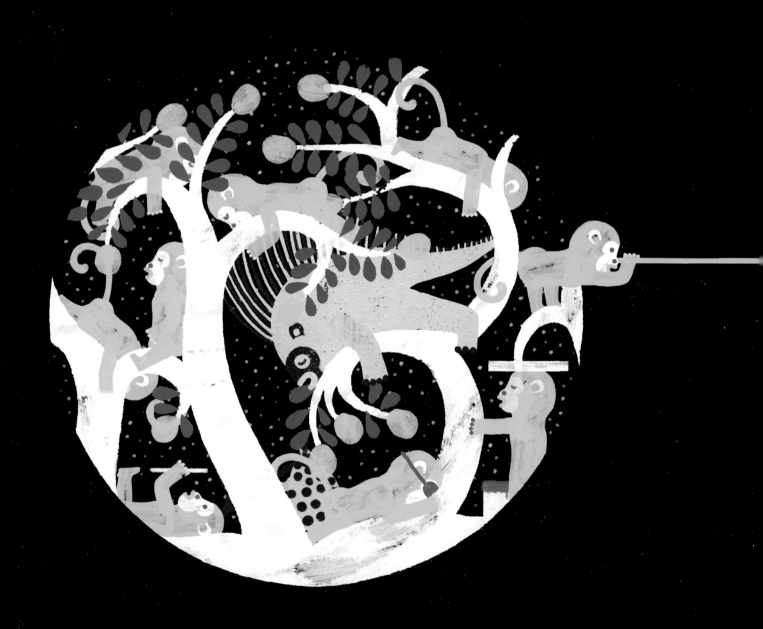

Good night.